Kids Like Us

by CAROLE LEXA SCHAEFER

Illustrated by PIERR MORGAN

VIKING

Fwoom!

As the yellow bus pulls away,

on a gray drizzle day,

who takes off in it?

Riders like us!

"Honk!" "Beep! Beep!" "Let's go!"

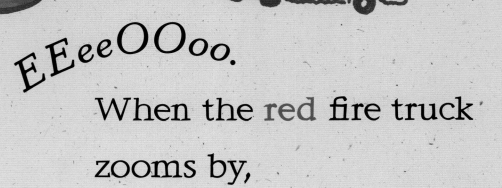

EEeeOOoo.

When the red fire truck

zooms by,

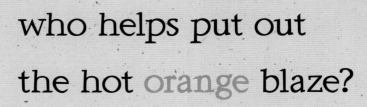

who helps put out
the hot orange blaze?

Firefighters like us!

"SHOOSHHH!"

"Squirt, squirt!"

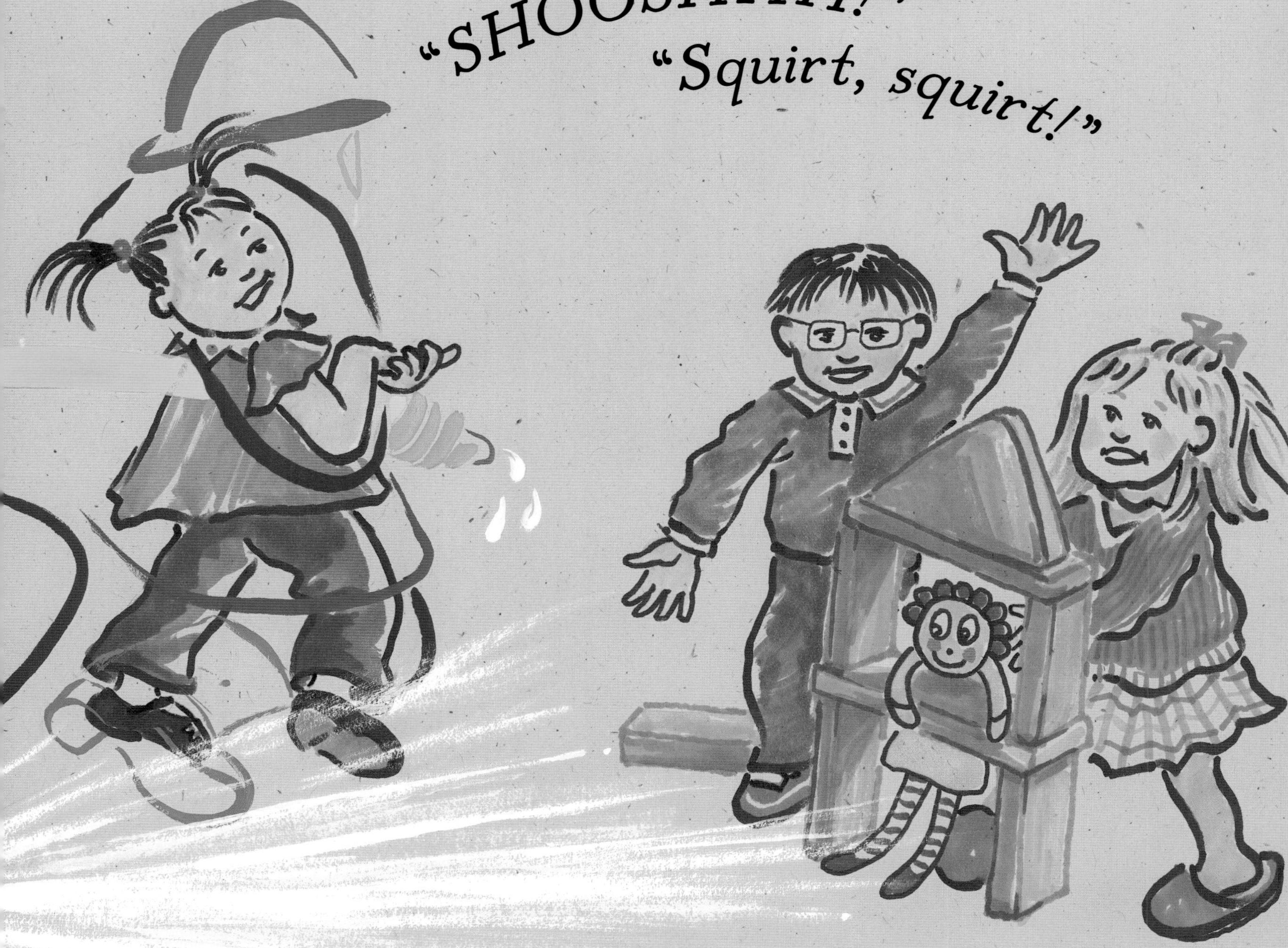

"Baby's safe!"

Sizzle Hiss.

Down in the green steamy jungle,

where wildness grows,

who—big or small—

is the loudest?

Dinos like us!

"*WUFFLE!*"

Whooosh!

As the purple curtain

blows aside,

who pops out

to put on a silly show?

Clowns like us!

"Yee-ha!"

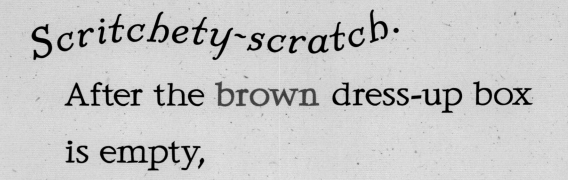

Scritchety-scratch.

After the brown dress-up box

is empty,

who meets there for supper?

Bears like us!

"Crunch."

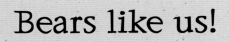

Ring-a-ding!

The bell rings—cleanup time.

Who puts the rainbow dress-ups away?

Knights and princesses like us!

"Kind Sir."

"M'Lady."

"Your Majesty."

Pit . . . pat . . . putt.

As the music of the gray drizzle stops,

who marches out

to the beat of their own big band

into the blue sky day?

Kids like us!

"Bim-bam!"

"Boom-bang!"

"Bye-bye."

From Carole and Pierr to kids like us:

Mary, Dave, and Judy; Susan, Joff, and Tam;

and especially Tracy and Nancy

Viking

Published by Penguin Group

Penguin Young Readers Group, 345 Hudson Street, New York, New York 10014, U.S.A.

Penguin Group (Canada), 90 Eglinton Avenue East, Suite 700, Toronto, Ontario, Canada M4P 2Y3 (a division of Pearson Penguin Canada Inc.)

Penguin Books Ltd, Registered Offices: 80 Strand, London WC2R 0RL, England

First published in 2008 by Viking, a division of Penguin Young Readers Group

1 3 5 7 9 10 8 6 4 2

LIBRARY OF CONGRESS CATALOGING-IN-PUBLICATION DATA

Schaefer, Carole Lexa.

Kids like us / by Carole Lexa Schaefer ; illustrated by Pierr Morgan.

p. cm.

Summary: On a gray drizzly day, school children imagine themselves as many different things, from firefighters to dinosaurs to kings and queens.

ISBN 978-0-670-06290-4 (hardcover)

[1. Schools—Fiction. 2. Play—Fiction. 3. Imagination—Fiction.] I. Morgan, Pierr, ill. II. Title.

PZ7.S3315Ki 2008   [E]—dc22   2007038221

Set in Godlike and Colwell italic   Manufactured in China   Book design by Nancy Brennan